SEYNA RYTES

The Note

A Wholesome Muslim Romance

First edition

This book was professionally typeset on Reedsy.
Find out more at reedsy.com

In the name of God, the Most Gracious, the Most Merciful.

JazakAllah Layla.

"He placed between you affection..."

[Quran 30:21]

Contents

Foreword

Please see below for a brief glossary of Arabic and Islamic terms used throughout this book. These definitions reflect the meaning I intended when using the words.

GLOSSARY OF COMMON ARABIC/MUSLIM TERMS

JazakAllah: May God reward you

JazakAllahu Hayran: May God reward you with goodness

Ramadan: Islamic month of fasting, prayer, reflection, community

Hijab: Common way of describing Muslim women's head covering

Hijabi: Muslim woman who wears a hijab

Quran: Central religious text in Islam

Eid: Name of the two major Muslim religious holidays

Eid Al Adha: Islamic holiday that honors the willingness of Ibrahim to sacrifice his son Ismael as an act of obedience to God

Allah: Arabic word for God

Insha Allah: God willing

Mosque/Masjid: Muslim place of worship

Dua: prayer

A Salaam U Aleykum: May peace be upon you. Muslim greeting

Wu Aleykum A Salaam: And unto you peace. Reply to Muslim greeting

Astaghfirullah: I seek forgiveness in God

Alhamdulilah: Praise be to God

SubhanAllah: Glory to God

Subhana Wa Ta'ala: May He be praised and exalted

Ya Rabbi: Oh, Lord / Oh My God

Abaya: Dress worn by women in parts of the Islamic world

Habibi (to a male) / Habibti (to a female): Literal: the one who is loved

Allahu Akbar: God is the greatest

Mabruk: Congratulations

Ameen: Amen

Imam: The person who leads prayers in a mosque / the leader of a Muslim community

Daara: Traditional Mauritanian male outfit

Preface

I grew up reading romance that was written by and intended for an audience that does not resemble me. Which was fine: I fell for the love stories, not the characters' skin color or their socioeconomic status. (I do remember a certain blue eyed, blond Russian Prince, though...)

I believe the topics of love and human connection to be universal. BUT, there are matters specific to each group of people. Whether because of their ethnical background, their age, the times in which they live, or their religion, to name only a few.

The story you're about to read deals with the universal themes of young love, but it also specifically addresses matters that young Muslims face when wanting to enter into marriage. Such as abstinence, desire, the building of trust, the practical issues that come with working on blending two lives together, the difficulty of navigating courtship while staying true to one's principles.

So, whoever you are, dear reader, I hope you enjoy Hadeel and Habib's love story, because after all that's all it is: a romance.

Acknowledgement

A thousand thank yous to my sisters of the trade, my tribe, Team Seyna & Imani! YOU ROCK.

I

GHOSTS OF RAMADANS PAST

1

HIGH SCHOOL

HADEEL

"I guess you're not coming to the mall tomorrow, huh?" My best friend, Huda, questions, brow raised, hand on her hip. Acting like an absolute pest in front of our group of girlfriends, who exchange catty smiles and avoid my gaze.

I stare at her with incredulity. Her beautiful porcelain skin, delicate features, nymph like form and long ebony hair. The dark eyes that used to convey so much warmth and affection for me...

"No, I'm not interested in aimlessly hanging out at the mall during *Ramadan*, and that's not new," I retort, gathering my things to walk away from them.

I'm so done with this mess! Ever since I made the decision to start wearing hijab, Huda's been an absolute PITA. Nothing like the girl I've known since childhood, been to *Quran* school with every weekend for more than a decade and had countless sleepovers with. She used to be my forever buddy, my ride or die. The friend with whom I spoke for hours about our dreams and aspirations. How we'd grow up to be fancy, fashionista *hijabis* and not dress boringly. How we'd go all out and decorate our homes for *Eid*. Wear amazing gowns for our weddings. Marry the most handsome, loving, successful brothers. Travel the world. Make the cutest babies and have it all: a great education, fulfilling career and happy marriage and family.

I guess I was supposed to ask for her permission or something! I really don't get what Huda's problem is: I'm still the exact same person, not the stuffy character she's portraying me to be. *I felt the urge to abide by a precept of my religion, sue me!* That doesn't mean I'm labelling anyone as a bad Muslim or thinking of myself as better. Rolling my eyes, I pick up my pace, in the direction of the classroom and ignore the snickering drama queens at my back.

May Allah help me! I'm trying to stay strong and calm. Strong in my decision to abide by the dress code prescribed in the *Quran*, and calm in the face of ignorance and lack of understanding.

Ask anyone, they'll tell you: high school's a nightmare only made bearable by your tribe, the close circle you choose and build for yourself. Well, mine has disintegrated the minute I walked into school with a piece of cloth wrapped around my head. First, it was the judgmental looks from the staff and pretty much every student from freshmen to my fellow seniors. Then, came the pointed fingers and guffaws from ignoramus kids. All that, I could handle because I had the support of the people who mattered to me: my family and closest friends. At least, I thought I did... till Huda started going all Mean Girl on me.

I plop into a chair, throw my messenger bag on the desk and lay my head and crossed forearms on it. *This too shall pass, Insha Allah.* Pulling out my textbook, a folded piece of paper falls on the tabletop. Without giving it much thought, my fingers

4

automatically open what appears to be a note with a single sentence scribbled in neat handwriting: 'I think you're beautiful in hijab.' *What?! Who slipped this in my bag? How?!! When did they...?* My eyes scan the classroom for any suspicious face, but there's not much to work with. The other kids are still scattered in small groups, some goofing around, others typing away on their phones. No one is paying me a speck of attention. Of course, now that I've been the new distraction for a week, my oddity status has lessened.

This is either invited the sweetest or crappiest thing anyone has ever done to me, if it's some kind of joke. I look toward Huda and find her in deep discussion with the girls. They're probably planning *our* usual Saturday afternoon hangout at the mall... without me. So, it's definitely not a note of encouragement from her or any of my former besties.

My gaze falls back on the piece of paper, rereading the kind words, then roam around the room once more. All I see is indifferent, bored faces and huddles of teenagers messing around during the short amount of time we have left before our teacher comes in. Well, not exactly all of them... there's someone sitting quietly on the opposite side of the room, head turned toward the window. His beautiful profile pulls my eyes like it always does. Habib Adam, my lifelong crush. The tall, reserved, handsome boy who barely knows I exist.

Habib is, like Huda and me, one of the few Muslim kids in our school. We live in Marina, a tiny Central California town, so there's only a small number of us. Just enough that we have a mosque and *Quran* school. Our families all know each other. We grew up hanging out every weekend at the *Masjid* and being invited over to a different family's throughout Ramadan. That means I've always had Habib on my radar. From when he was a scrawny kid with beautiful almond shaped eyes, to the time he transformed into every high school girl's fantasy.

As ever, I try my best to not let my gaze linger over his handsome features, soft, deep brown eyes and warm smile. I try not to imagine how it would feel to have his low baritone address me in an intimate manner: maybe during an hour-long conversation over the phone before bedtime. I REALLY try, and I make *Dua* for *Allah* to help me stay firm in my resolve, but it's so hard! Habib is just too darn perfect. He's a practicing Muslim, and a kind, reserved, insanely attractive young man, with *Insha Allah* a bright future ahead of him. An excellent student, athletic, no trouble type of guy. None of us, girls in his age range, would mind receiving his attentions.

So, no: as much as I wish this beautiful note came from Habib, I won't fool myself. Although, there was that one time... That magical afternoon when the stars aligned and gifted me a stolen moment with the boy who makes my heart beat faster.

***

That was a year ago, on a rainy day where my car wouldn't start, and everyone had already left campus. My parents were held up at work and my sister at university. I was waiting under the admin building for Triple A. Annoyed to be stuck in school hours after people went home, worried about my car and altogether having a crappy day. I was completely unaware of my surroundings when a gentle voice called my name.

"Hadeel."

I startled and turned around to face... a gray sweatshirt covered torso. My eyes travelled up to meet the kind gaze of the tall adolescent I'd known for most of my life.

"Oh, hey Habib. *A Salaam U Aleykum.* What are you still doing here?" I asked.

"*Wu Aleykum A Salaam.* I was going to ask you the same thing. I just finished practice." He replied, dropping his gym bag at his feet.

"Oh OK. My car won't start and my family's not available to come get me. I'm waiting for Triple A." I explained with a shoulder shrug, playing with the loose end of my hijab.

Habib gave me a head nod and posted himself at a foot's distance.

"I'll wait with you, then I'll drive you home." He declared.

"No, you don't have to do that. I'm sure the mechanic will give me a ride."

"It's fine, sister." He deadpanned.

Sister, at this word I was reminded of my position. Habib wasn't offering to wait with me because he was being friendly or anything personal, it was simply a good deed. After a full day of schoolwork and hours of basketball practice, he still found it in him to be a good Samaritan. *Ugh, so annoying!*

We stood in silence in the rain, surrounded by the sounds of nature. I was all at once tickled and stressed beyond measure to do or say the wrong thing. As always, Habib appeared to be poised and self-assured. The very definition of the strong, silent type. I tried my best to keep my eyes away from him, as if I wouldn't have been able to draw every single one of his facial traits had I had the talent. The fight to not inhale his clean scent was also strenuous: I could tell he was fresh out of the shower, smelling of citrus and woodsy aromas. And standing next to each other, it was beyond difficult not to compare our heights and frames. His tall, athletic one and my medium size, curvy body. How many times had I fantasized about how it would feel to be Habib's fiancée, or his wife and snuggle up against his tall form? *Astaghfirullah!* I kept repeating to myself, fighting to keep

7

my mind away from thoughts that could lead to no good.

Of course, Habib was completely unaffected. He waited with me like the gentleman he is, spoke to the Triple A mechanic and gave me a silent ride home. End of story. Well, almost... If I thought it was hard resisting his pull, standing outdoors at school, under the admin building porch. I was completely unprepared for the close quarters of his pick-up. The air was saturated with his smell. Not only the fragrance of his body soap, after shave, cologne or whatever was turning me into goo, but the very scent that was attached to his skin. I also tried not to notice Habib's long, elegant fingers on the steering wheel, his strong body sitting at just a foot's distance from me but failed... *SubhanAllah.*

And of course, once we made it to my house, he insisted on coming inside and waiting for my dad to report on his exchange with the Triple A mechanic. I remember my father watching us with an amused glint in his observant gaze, but *Hamdullah* he never teased me about it.

Yeah, so the note is definitely not from Habib, despite my wildest hopes. As the teacher enters the classroom, I fold it back and tuck it in my pencil pouch. Hurrying to shoot a text to my sister about the crazy thing I need to tell her about.

***

"Don't worry about Huda," my older sister, Halima reassures me.

"Yeah, easy for you to say. It's not your best friend who's suddenly become your frenemy."

She shakes her head in her habitual fashion, when implying I'm a dramatic teenager.

"I'm serious, Lima! It's like no one at school speaks to me anymore."

"Exaggerate much?" Halima cocks her head to the side.

"Barely: I refuse to count the teachers and school counsellor."

She burst with laughter and I can't help but smile. *Alhamdulilah* for my big sister, my true best friend. She's always here to uplift me and talk things through.

"Give it time. Huda is pissed because you guys talked about wearing hijab forever, and you went and did it without her."

"But she wasn't even in town, she was on vacation in Lebanon!" I protest.

"Doesn't matter. All she sees is her bestie took a major step and left her behind."

I stay quiet for a few seconds, mulling over Halima's words. When she puts it that way...?

"My point is: don't worry. You made an amazing decision, *Insha Allah* everything will work out."

"You really think so?" I ask, biting on my thumbnail.

"I know so!" She gives me a reassuring wink.

My mind goes to the note and I jump from Halima's bed, rushing to my bedroom, throwing over my shoulder: "Oh My God, I need to show you something!"

After frantically rummaging through my pencil pouch, I find the note, read it again, just to remind myself how wonderful the words are, hold it to my chest for a few seconds, and walk back to my sister's room, handing it to her.

"Here, read."

"What do we have here?" She mumbles before her eyes open wide. "Wow! Who is this from? Why have we been talking about Huda? This is so much more interesting."

I giggle before answering: "I don't know. I found it in my

9

bag when I was pulling my textbook out. What do you think it means?"

"What do you think, dingdong? There's obviously someone who likes you, headscarf and all." She's smiling broadly, happy for me.

"You have to help me figure out who it is, Lima!"

"Girl, I don't have time for your high school drama," she laughs.

"This is not drama, it's dreamy," I sigh and lay back on the bed, holding the note up with my arms extended, making my sister laugh even harder.

***

The rest of the school year is mostly uneventful. I slowly regain my status as just another normal kid with her own weirdness.

Huda and I progressively bridge the gap between us. It starts with a few words, family visits, *Iftars* at the *Masjid*, till finally we reconcile on *Eid*.

Habib stays a far away, unattainable fantasy.

My only regret from that year is I never found out who was the author of the note...

*** ***

HABIB

Get it together, man! I run a hand down my face, frustrated with myself. I see how people have been treating Hadeel, talking behind her back and staring. And it kills me not to be able to offer her more help.

At least, none of the guys has dared doing it again when I'm around. All it took was putting one stupid moron in his place.

"What's up with the baggy clothes and headgear, man? This chick used to be hot," the pimply adolescent commented as Hadeel passed our group.

I pinned him with a lethal glare and walked up to tower over him feet to feet, standing to my full stature and asking in a deceivingly calm tone: "what did you say?"

He started stuttering: "I was just messing around, man."

I dipped my chin and growled in his face: "you don't talk about her. You don't look at her."

He nodded frantically and scurried away. I let my eyes roam through the group of jocks. Some met my gaze with surprise, others looked away, but I was pretty sure my message came across loud and clear. No one was to mess with Hadeel.

The guys know me: they know my brand of quiet. I don't talk much or fool around. I keep to myself and my close circle. Play ball, focus on school, hang out a bit. My attention is on my *Deen*, my loved ones and working toward my future. I'm not into any type of mess: drugs, alcohol, girls, easy money. None of that interests me. Well, that's not exactly true about the girls. I've had my eye on Hadeel for a while now. I guess I've had a fondness for her since we were kids. With her big, bright smiles and easy conversation. She was always the one to come pull me out of my corner to play with everyone else. The one to tease me and break through my shell. Things started changing a few years back. I guess growing up has carved a rift between us. There are

11

no more games of tag to pull me into. *Dang, she can't even take me by the hand anymore.*

I make a short *Dua* for peace of mind and strength. I want to help the girl I like, but can't get too close to her. She's just too tempting with her lively eyes, full mouth and perfect body. No wonder I'm constantly tongue-tied around Hadeel. I take in a deep inhale and put my trust in *Allah Subhana Wa Ta'ala.* Serenity and clarity will come. In time.

2

COLLEGE

HADEEL

"You coming?" Huda asks, checking her reflection in our entrance mirror. She fixes her dust rose jersey hijab and turns around to make sure her maxi dress falls right.

I raise an eyebrow in a *'really?'* fashion.

"Girl, please. It's after Maghreb, we're just going to Starbucks. Live a little."

"*Alh*amdullah, I live plenty, thank you very much. And going to Starbucks with your crush and a bunch of other couples doesn't seem like the best Ramadan-post-Iftar activity. So, if you'll excuse me."

"Pfff, Malik isn't my crush. I just think he's cute, funny and perfect for a little after-hours entertainment." Huda answers.

I shake my head with a smile, stuff my earbuds back in and redirect my gaze to the textbook open on my bed. The sounds of nature playing from some hour-long Youtube video mostly drown out the click of Huda's heels and her shuffling around our dorm room. Still, I can't wait till she leaves and I can really

13

focus on my studying.

We broke our fast about an hour ago, *SubhnAllah*. We prayed together and refreshed, and now I'm planning on a few hours of course review before I read Quran and crash. The loss of energy due to fasting is no joke, *MashAllah!* Or maybe it's just me who's a granny... Which, according to Huda, is facts.

Finding it impossible to concentrate, I pause my white noise and stretch my limbs before plopping up on an elbow. Pretending to check my nails, I ask in a voice too heavily infused with bored indifference to be genuine: "Who's going?"

Huda tilts her head to the side, smirking at me. "It thought it wasn't a good idea to hang out with one's crush during Ramadan?" She teases.

I smirk right back at my bestie, who knows me too well. Then I come out with it, asking: "fine, is he going?"

Huda watches me for a beat before answering with a question of her own: "would that change your decision?"

I shake my head firmly. *Nope, I'm determined to not only observe a physical fast but, more than anything, work on my character. And resisting the pull of a certain brown-eyed boy is definitely part of the challenge I want to best, Insha Allah.*

"Not that I know of. You know Habib's as much of a goodie two shoes as you are. You two probably have the exact same program for the night," Huda mumbles through pursed lips, busy applying gloss. "OK, I'm out of here. Last chance..." she trails off.

I shake my head again, wishing her a good time. When the door clicks behind her, I slump back on my full-size bed, eyes to the ceiling. *I'm not sure much studying will actually get done tonight...* A knock at the door interrupts my lazy thoughts.

"Yeah?"

The handle goes down and a low masculine voice greets: "*A Salaam U Aleykum.*"

"*Wu Aleykum A Salaam,*" I respond, swiftly sitting up straight. *Alhamdullah,* I have my hair wrapped up in a scarf. It's not my usual full head and cleavage covering, but it'll do. It's Friday night, I'm in my pink flannel pajamas, alone in my room. If someone felt this was the time to come over, they'll just have to deal.

Habib pokes his head inside the room...

"How are you, sister? Sorry to bother."

Ugh, sister!

"I'm good *Hamdullah,* and you? No problem." I respond, my voice turning guarded, as always when I'm in this man's presence. Unrequited infatuation and all that...

He stands at the entrance to the room, leaving the door wide open, hands behind his back. Appearing to be waiting for something... His eyes roam around the space, jumping from one wall to another, going over our framed Islamic quotes, decorative posters, the flowerpots on the windowsill and quickly turn away from any personal item they encounter. Huda's robe draped over her office chair. My romance novels stacked on a bookshelf. When his gaze falls on the small frame resting on my nightstand, the reminder that a kind soul took the time to send me support when I needed it the most, Habib does a double take and I scrutinize his handsome features in search of the answer to the question that's been haunting me for years now. Was he the one who wrote the note? Habib's expression quickly turns blank and I guess I've imagined the glint in his eye. *Yeah, Mr. Halal here definitely didn't write and sneak me a note that said I was beautiful.*

15

I have no clue what he's doing here, and my curiosity makes it even more difficult than usual to avert my gaze. The man is gorgeous for Heaven's sake! Even taller than when he played basketball back in high school, probably close to six feet five, now. He also filled in nicely. The white, embroidered, loose fitting linen ensemble he's wearing can't hide the lines of his defined muscles. His short, cropped hair still curls in dark waves. His smooth looking skin, a deep brown tone. The warm eyes, masculine nose, full lips and square jaw reminiscent of his Moor ancestors. *Astaghfirullah, I need to get a grip!*

The other thing that hasn't changed is his quietness. This guy is the undefeated universal champ of the silent game, *MashAllah*.

"Uh, do you need something?" I finally inquire.

Habib's surprised gaze briefly meets mine before evading again. I do the same and lower my eyes to his feet. He's wearing leather sandals and even his feet are attractive... *Darn it!*

"Hum... Huda said you needed help with homework?" He explains in an uncertain tone.

I will cut a sister!

"She probably misunderstood. I'm fine. Thanks for stopping by." I give him a tight-lipped smile, not about to get trapped in one of Huda's crazy plans.

Habib hovers at the door for a few more seconds before shrugging his massive shoulders.

"OK, I'll leave you to it, then. Good luck, *A Salaam U Aleykum*." He waves, lingering for a beat.

"*Wu Aleykum A Salaam*, thanks again." This time, I try infusing warmth into my voice.

Habib gifts me a small grin and walks away. Once more, the door closes, and I fall back on the mattress. This time, my thoughts are not filled with sleepiness or lack of motivation for schoolwork, but the familiar tug of longing. *I gotta shake off my feelings for this guy.* Habib is not interested. *Wallahi*, all he seems to care about is his family, friends, studies and basketball. I'm twenty years old, I'm ready to meet someone and start getting to know them. Build a relationship, a family. There's no way that will happen for as long as I'm hung up on some childhood fantasy. Huda has told me so and even Halima agrees with her... Soon, *Insha Allah*. When the time is right.

*** ***

HABIB

What an idiot! For God's sake, when will I learn to talk to this girl? It's not like I didn't know Huda was full of it. She pushes us in each other's arms every chance she gets. And I know for a fact Hadeel is a brilliant student, she didn't need my help with homework.

I saw the irritation in her eyes. I'm losing her and I only have myself to blame. I'm noticing how other guys on campus look at her, some even bold enough to approach my Hadeel. I know she's not interested in dating, but some day, some brother will start courting her, and then what? I have no right, no claim to her.

Ya Rabbi, I've been praying to outgrow this rigidity around Hadeel. Tried overcoming it, but I'm stuck. I can't look at her, listen to her melodious voice, hear her beautiful laugh without getting hard. I avoid Hadeel in order to fight my *Nafs,* and it's a vicious circle. The more attracted and infatuated I become, the more I need to keep my distance to stay respectful and *Halal* in my thoughts, words and actions.

I don't see a way out of this. We're not ready to get together. At least, I'm not yet the man I know Hadeel deserves. I want to be financially independent from my family, able to support her, whether she needs it or not. Able to provide for the family we'll build together. I especially want to be ready to take on any challenges life throws our way.

May *Allah* help us...

II

PRESENT DAY

3

THE MEET

HADEEL

"I know we haven't seen each other much, lately." I tell Reda, the man I've been going out with for a few months now. "I'm trying, but you know we're in the middle of a deal. I can't fast, run to a meeting on the other side of town, then join you for *Iftar*. Just give me till Saturday."

I feel bad having to decline another one of his invitations. Especially, since I know Reda's busy too, and makes seeing me a priority on his schedule.

"OK," he grumbles in a disappointed tone, and I picture his handsome face marred by a frown. Mouth pinched, thick dark brows furrowed and long finger pushing back his black framed glasses in a gesture of irritation. Jet black curly hair and olive skin tone making the dark green of his eyes come out in contrast.

"Thank you for understanding, *A Salaam U Aleykum*," I bid Reda goodbye and hang up, shaking my head.

He's a great guy. Kind, good looking, a practicing Muslim and a successful lawyer. Everyone tells me how lucky I am to have met Reda. And I know he's serious about us, but I'm just not sure I'm there yet. We met through common friends at a dinner party and immediately hit it off with a natural camaraderie. A few days after the dinner, I was surprised when my girlfriend, our hostess, told me Reda had asked for my number. I honestly had more of a friendship vibe from our encounter, but I wasn't about to turn my back on a potential match. Twenty-five-year-old, busy consultant at a risk advisory firm, living an ocean away from my family and friends, my opportunities to meet potential life partners are limited. And Reda is great... on paper, I'm just not sure we fit. The more time we spend together, the more I question the depth of our connection. *Ya Rabbi!*

I rub a hand over my face, shaking off my grim thoughts and step into the reception area of the Soho Mayfair social club. I'm meeting a client to discuss the next phase in our current assignment for his small tech firm. This is one of the many facets of London I love: conducting business in the refined setting of private members' clubs. Taking the corporate world outside of conference rooms.

"I'm here to meet Mr. Greenfield," I let the hostess know.

As she's about to let me in, a deep masculine voice calls from behind me: "Hadeel? Hadeel Seydi?"

I turn around and come face to face with my long-lost youth acquaintance, Habib Adam. We must be wearing mirror expressions of incredulity, stunned to find ourselves in the same place after years of not seeing each other, and so far from home. I giggle, my seven-year-old-self coming out to play at the sight of her favorite person in the world. Hearing the silly sound I just uttered, I know I need to rein it in before high school Hadeel pokes her head out.

Clearing my throat, I use my best grown-up conversation

voice: "Habib Adam, it's nice to see you, brother."

"Same here, *MashAllah*. What a small world," he answers, watching me with rapt attention. His smile not too forthright, but with a definite glint of interest in his gaze. Which could just be due to curiosity...

"It is, indeed. Who'd think two Central Coast kids would find themselves in the same prestigious London club?" I tease, showing off my adulting skills like nobody's business.

Habib's low chuckle lets me know the brother has changed quite a bit. His rich brown eyes haven't once wavered from mine since we've made contact. He's smiling broadly and standing at a respectable, but close distance. What happened to quiet, reserved Habib?

He shakes his head with incredulity.

"This is crazy, *MashAllah*. Are you a member?"

"No, I have a meeting with a client who is. What about you?"

"I have a meeting too, and I'm a member."

He's just as tall and handsome as I remember. Towering over me, dressed in an impeccably cut charcoal gray suit. Almond shaped eyes twinkling with excitement.

"What time's your meeting?" Habib asks, his strong, white teeth biting down on his full bottom lip.

Asthaghfirullah!

I clear my throat and respond with a hint of iciness: "I actually need to get going. It was nice seeing you again, Habib. *A Salaam*...
"

"Whoa, not so fast," he interrupts. "I want to hear everything about what you're been up to. Let's exchange numbers."

I hesitate for a beat, before nodding in agreement and we trade business cards. Gaze averted, I throw Habib a rushed goodbye over my shoulder and hurry inside the club to the table where

23

my client is waiting, bringing my full attention to the matter at hand and pushing away thoughts of the darn blast from the past!

***

"You'll never guess who I bumped into today," I send an audio message in my group chat with my sister and Huda, as soon as I exit the Soho Mayfair.

Huda is the first one to reply. Newborn baby or not, that girl always makes time for a juicy gossip.

'WHO?!' she texts in all caps.

'HABIB!!' I reply in stride.

'Say *Wallah*!!'

'WALLAHI!!!' I type back, snickering at the tone of our exchange. In the span of a short text message exchange, we've definitely regressed by a solid decade.

Walking toward the subway station, my heels clicking on the cobbled pavement, I pick up the phone on the first ring and hold it in front of my face for our group video call. I love how Halima has no time for Huda and I's long dragged back and forth.

"*A Salaam U Aleykum.* You lyin'!"

I let out a snort and cover my mouth, looking around to see if anyone caught that, but thankfully the British are as unintrusive as ever.

"No, I'm not lying, crazy. We just met at a private members' club. And I think he lives here..."

"Oh My God!" Huda exclaims. "We've found Habib again!"

We all laugh and my sister goes on: "what about Reda?"

"What about him?" I ask back, sobering up.

Huda cocks her head to the side in her signature 'don't be daft'

24

move.

"Guys, I just thought it was crazy and I wanted to share. That's all. You can't compare the guy I've been seeing for six months with some old crush."

If they could exchange a knowing look through their phone screens, that's what would happen right now.

Huda goes: "uh-huh."

While my sister pacifies me with an unconvinced: "of course."

I roll my eyes and push on: "I'm sure he won't even call."

This time, they exchange bugged-eye expressions.

"Back up. He won't *call?*..." Lima questions.

"Yeah, we exchanged business cards."

"Who initiated the exchange?" Huda, the Dr. Watson to Halima's Sherlock Holmes, asks.

"He asked for my number..." I grumble.

"Poor Reda," my sister shakes her head with a toothy grin.

Huda raises her arms, pumping the air in a ridiculous victory dance.

"I'm getting in the tube, it's gonna disconnect. I love you two, crazy people," I giggle before adding, "and nothing will happen with Habib," just before losing them.

Famous last words...

*** ***

HABIB

Hadeel Seydi. My Hadeel. *Alḥamdu lillāhi Rabbilʿālamīn!* What an amazing surprise!

For years, I've pushed her in a far corner of my mind. Only rarely revisiting the sweet memories of our childhood and my remembrance of the beautiful young woman she'd grown into. Like an old dream. A fantasy from another time and place. A time gone and lost, I'd never get again. I never expected to have such an encounter with Hadeel, the opportunity to see her again. To finally talk to her, now that I'm no longer a blubbering teenager.

What if she's married? Well, I checked and there was no ring on her finger. She could be engaged... Stop it, Habib! Allah Subhana Wa Ta'ala brought Hadeel back into your life. This can only be good, Insha Allah!

4

IFTAR

HADEEL

I walk into my apartment and get rid of my shoes at the entrance, making my way to the living room to sprawl out on the couch for a few minutes. *Hamdullah*, it was a long and productive day. Thank God, I was able to make *Salah* in my office. Glancing at my phone screen, I see it's twenty minutes to *Maghreb*. Time to go was up and prepare to break my fast.

An hour or so later, I'm all prayed up, fed and dozing off in front of the TV. One of the things I enjoy the most about living alone. As much as I miss being surrounded by my family and sharing the experience of the month of *Ramadan* with my community, the freedom of doing things at my own pace is invaluable. I'm so deliciously groggy, all worries about my lack of compatibility with Reda or the surprise meet with Habib are just vague, hovering thoughts at the border of my consciousness. I'm about to completely drift off when my phone rings.

"Hello," I mumble into the receiver.

"Hadeel?" Habib asks in his low timbre and I straighten up, wide awake.

"Hey, *A Salaam U Aleykum*."

"*Wu Aleykum A Salaam.* Is this a good time?"

"Yeah, yeah. Of course."

"You're not busy with *Iftar*?"

"No, I'm done eating."

"Good, good."

He's quiet for a few seconds.

"It was really nice seeing you again today. I'd love to spend some time together." When I don't immediately respond, he adds: "to catch up and stuff."

Of course, two people who've known each other for most of their lives, and find themselves living in the same city. That just makes sense.

"Yes, of course. I'd like that."

"Perfect," Habib proceeds, "*Iftar* tomorrow?"

What?!

Stunned silent, it takes me a little while to reply: "uh, sure. What do you have in mind?"

"There's a great *Halal* Chinese next to my place in Queensbridge. I think you'll enjoy it."

I burst out laughing and Habib asks with a smile in his voice: "what's funny?"

"The fact we have the option to eat *Halal* Chinese, when we grew up in a town where there wasn't even a *Halal* store or restaurant."

"True that," he chuckles in a low rumble that does things to my belly.

Oh boy...

"OK, text me the details, please."

28

"I will. Have a good night," his voice dips by an octave in a warm farewell.

And it's only after we've hang up that I remember I promised Reda to meet over the weekend, but just made plans to see Habib on a work night.

***

"How's Huda?" Habib enquires with an amused smile, making my eyes drift to the assortment of dishes on our table.

Roast duck, Chow Mein, spring rolls, fried rice... there's way too much food for the two of us, but he insisted on making me try the house specials.

"She's still the same, except married and a mom now."

"Wow, *MashAllah.* That's great."

"She lives in Manchester. Actually, we moved here together."

He nods with interest.

"How long ago was that?"

"Going on two years, now. We did our Masters at the London Business School, found jobs." I mark a pause before adding: "and Huda found a husband."

Habib watches me closely from under his thick eyelashes.

"You didn't?"

I smile and shake my head. "If I had a husband, I don't think we'd be sharing an *Iftar* meal at a Chinese restaurant."

"No?"

"I would have invited you over, made a dozen dishes and you'd spent the evening chatting with my husband."

"Sounds like a lot less fun," he says in a low voice, his gaze capturing mine.

"I have someone, though," I blurt out, using Reda to break

the spell.

"Oh," Habib utters, his thick brows coming together in a furrow. "You're engaged?" He asks bluntly.

"Uh, not exactly. I'm seeing someone and he's made his intentions clear."

"I see," He states, expression still dark. "What are your intentions for him?"

My mouth falls open at his intrusive question. I can't reconcile this man with the quiet, reserved boy I grew up knowing. Such assurance in his speech, such confidence in his demeanor! Habib has truly grown into his full potential as a man.

When he texted me our meeting time, he insisted on getting my address and came to get me in front of my building. We drove in an amicable back and forth of questions about our families, the people we knew in common from back home and what our lives were like now.

Habib is a senior analyst at a financial firm and seems to love his work, his apartment and all around his life in the U.K. He didn't mention a woman, but handsome as he is and with his knew found swagger, I doubt he lacks feminine attention. He's not a player, though. At least that's not the vibe I perceive. More of a self-assured guy, who knows his mind.

I've loved our easy exchange, till the delicate subject of the status of my relationship with Reda comes up.

"Uh..." I sigh loudly, pushing back my impulse to tell Habib off. "I don't see myself with him in the long term."

"Does he know that?"

"I haven't been forthright."

"Is there a reason you haven't."

"I guess I don't want to hurt him?" I formulate as a question. "And, I was giving things time, to see if maybe my feelings would change." I admit to both Habib and myself. Being honest for the first time about my true sentiment for Reda.

Habib nods solemnly before adding: "you need to tell him."

"I know." I say quietly. "I will," I add with a sad smile. Already dreading the conversation that can only hurt the ego, if not the feelings of a good man.

"It's for the best."

"I know, Habib."

He stares at me with intensity, brown eyes saying a thousand words his mouth won't utter. He nods pensively.

"OK, we can revisit the subject after you've spoken to him," is his insane comment.

What is happening?! I stare at Habib mouth agape and he winks at me with mischief. I definitely want to have some of whatever they gave him to turn the shy boy into a deliciously cocky man.

Probably sensing I'm this close to bolting, Habib changes the trajectory of the conversation: "any plans for *Eid*?"

"I'm going home," I answer with a grin, my nerves relaxing a bit.

"Me too," he smiles back.

"I try flying back every couple of months, my schedule permitting."

He nods. "Yeah, it's about the same for me. When are you going?"

I let him know when I'm flying out of London, and we continue chatting, the earlier tension almost completely dissipated.

"I had a great time, *MashAllah*."

Habib stands a few steps below me on my front porch stairs, making our eyes level.

"Me too, *Hamdullah*," I respond in kind.

"I'll see you soon, *A Salaam U Aleykum,*" he affirms and turns on his heels with a bright smile.

"*Wu Aleykum Asalaam,*" I tell his departing form.

Lord have mercy.

*** ***

<u>HABIB</u>

"*A Salaam U Aleykum,* Ma. How are you?"

"*Wu Aleykum A Salaam.* Great, *Hamdullah,* and you, my son?"

I take a deep inhale, my face split by a giant grin, trying to rein in my excitement.

"Is Baba home?"

"Yeah, let me get him."

I hear her call in the background.

"Bilal! It's Habib on the phone!"

I shake my head, chuckling: my mom, always yelling.

"*A Salaam U Aleykum,* Habib my boy, how are you?"

"I'm great, Baba. Could you please put the phone on speaker?"

I hear a bit of ruffling, before he speaks again: "we're here. What's up?" Straight to the point, just like me.

"There's a woman I'm interested in courting."

They both fall silent, before my mom lets out a shaky laugh.

"*Alhamdulilah!* My son is getting married! Who is she?" My mother starts rattling away.

"Ma, calm down. I haven't even spoken to her parents yet, and actually she might be in talks with another brother already."

"Pff," Mama brushes off. "When I met your dad, he was courting someone and I was talking to three brothers, already. And look at us, thirty years happily married."

I hear my dad's amused chuckle.

"What does this young lady say about you courting her?"

I grab the back of my neck in a nervous gesture.

"Well, I haven't been totally forthright with her about my intentions."

"Come on, Habibi. You know better."

"Yeah... but she said she wasn't really into him and agreed to

33

stop things."

"OK. Why are you calling? You don't sound like it's advice you need."

My dad knows me like the back of his hand.

"It's Hadeel Seydi," I come out and admit.

Ma explodes in ululations, and Baba and I burst with laughter. My parents have long known about my soft spot for the youngest Seydi daughter. Our families are friends and always looked positively on the possibility of an us. But, we were simply too young when we both lived in California. *Insha Allah*, now is our time.

5

EID

HADEEL

One week. Seven entire days since my *Iftar* dinner with Habib, and not a call, a text, or a social media poke from the donkey of a man... *Astaghfirullah!*

Nothing. The same way he busted into my life; the man has disappeared into thin air.

I've debated with myself, Halima and Huda a ridiculous number of times about contacting him, but that just doesn't seem right. It would not sit well with my gut. I was fine! Living my life. I thought I'd forgotten all about the boy with the soulful eyes. Thought he was a vague memory from my past. Some silly youth nostalgia. How could I have been so wrong? How did I fool myself into thinking I was over Habib? The second I saw him on that afternoon in Mayfair, it was as if my heart had come back to life after a long slumber, and the feeling kept growing stronger. His phone call sent a myriad of butterflies into full motion in my stomach. Our shared *Iftar* was such a fun, reviving moment.

Sitting across the table from Habib, so close I could study all the tiny changes on his face. Letting the deep bass of his voice fill my ears and vibrate through my chest. Laughing at his jokes. Still amazed by this relaxed version of the stuffy kid from my memory.

I'd started hoping. I'd let myself reopen the door I thought was sealed forever. When Habib asked about Reda, I thought for sure he wanted to court me. *What an idiot!* This guy never had any interest in me, and now that he's turned into some kind of player, I was probably just another girl he made swoon. I think I hate men, *SubhanAllah*. Not all of them, though. Reda is a good guy. He just found himself entangled in my mess. I sigh deeply, mind filled with a combination of anger, self-loathing and sadness. I'm done wasting my time thinking of Habib... again. And I need to be honest with Reda.

***

"Just like that?" He asks in a glacial tone and I wish I could take his hand, comfort him.

"Not just like that. It... I always felt more friendship and affection for you than romantic feelings. I didn't know if that would change, but we've been seeing each other for months now."

Reda's gaze is furious. His nostrils flare with the deep, calming breaths he inhales. The man thinks I've been playing him.

"OK. We obviously were not on the same page. I was planning on asking you to come spend *Eid* at my parents' house. Glad we had this talk now."

I feel my eyes open wide. What could have given him the impression that our relationship was progressing toward and introduction to our families? I was always busy with work, not making much effort to see him...

"Again, I'm sorry. It was never my intent to lead you on."

"It's fine," his lips pull up in a tight smile. "*A Salaam U Aleykum.* I wish you the best."

"*Wu Aleykum A Salaam.* Thank you, me too Reda." I reply with fervor.

He gives me a brief nod and walks out of the small coffee shop in my street. I sigh with relief, feeling lighter now that it's done, but still feeling the knot Habib's disappearing act left in my belly. *I'll be OK, Insha Allah.* I got over him in the past, I can do it again. Especially now that I'm not stuck in the same small town, school or college as the prick. My only concern is the fact he told me he was going home for *Eid*, so I'm a bit apprehensive about my vacation next week. *But that's just silly!* I'll spend all my time with my parents, Halima and her family. Taking my nieces out and about and filling my belly with home cooked meals, there's little chance I'll even see Habib. It's just one week. *I'll be fine!*

***

"This is not OK. When was the last time we celebrated *Eid* together, dude?" I rile up Huda, making her snort.

"Well, maybe in a couple of years when Mustafa is older. I'm not flying with a newborn baby. Too much logistics to handle."

I laugh. "OK, well maybe I'll come spend the next *Eid* with you guys."

She squeals in my ear and I pull the phone away, a huge grin on my face.

"Dude..."

"Promise!"

"*Insha Allah.* Tell Kareem to prepare..."

I'm interrupted by a tap on my shoulder. I turn around and come face to face with Habib! *What. The. Hell.*

"Excuse me, Huda. I need to call you back."

I disconnect the call, slip the phone in my purse and cross my arms over my chest, one eyebrow raised.

"*Salaam*, brother." I greet him, my tone icy cold.

"*A Salaam U Aleykum.*" He responds with a bright smile.

Is this fool serious?

"What are you doing in my house?"

"Technically it's your parents house," he dares reply with a cheeky expression.

Oh no, he did not come to my childhood home, on Eid, in his stupid fancy outfit, all gorgeous dark skin and sparkly white teeth, to taunt and torture me with his delicious smelling cologne and muddle my thoughts!

"What. Are. You. Doing. Here. Habib." I enunciate between gritted teeth.

"I came to talk to you and pay my respects to your family."

We're standing in front of my parents' two-story house. Both still in our celebratory garments. Me, in a soft pink *Abaya* with delicate embroidery. Habib, in a navy blue tunic and assorted trousers that make him look dreamy, *Astaghfirullah!*

*** ***

<u>HABIB</u>

She's magnificent. All I want to do is throw Hadeel over my

38

shoulder and push a ring up her finger.

She's also upset... My mother warned me: you don't leave a woman alone to straighten her affairs without being clear on your intentions. But, it was also *Ramadan*. I didn't see myself staying in contact with Hadeel through the last ten days of the month and resisting the temptation to see her again.

"Hadeel, I know you haven't heard from me but..."

She interrupts me: "but what, Habib? You were too busy smoldering other women all over London? I don't know who you are. I haven't seen or spoken to you in five years, and here you come all smooth and intense, like some sort of *Halal* playboy."

Oh Lord...

"If you'll just let me explain, please."

"Explain what, Habib? You saw an old acquaintance in a city where we're far from our family and friends, and thought I could become your new plaything?" Hadeel's voice is hard and my own temper starts rising...

"Stop calling me a player. You said it yourself: you don't know me." I take a step closer, towering over her medium height. My nostrils flaring at the assault of her delicious perfume. I utter between gritted teeth: "I was waiting for the end of *Ramadan* to ask if you broke things off with your bloke."

She harrumphs, crossing her arms over her chest, but there's a

39

definite sparkle of interest in her gaze.

"And to ask for yours and your parents' permission to court you," I finish, bringing my hands to my hips in a challenging stance.

Hadeel's eyelids flutter in apparent confusion, before she asks in a whisper: "what?".

A cocky grin wipes off my thunderous expression. "You heard me. Is it over with him?"

She nods, lips parted in her surprise.

"Good. I'd be honored to express my intentions to your father."

Hadeel looks at me with wide eyes, my words slowly penetrating the fog of the past ten days she must have spent cursing me to hell.

When she finally speaks, her voice is calm, almost soft: "why? we only just got reacquainted."

I feel my lips crook up on one side. "You really have to ask?"

She nods, just once.

"Hadeel, you've never left my mind. ever since we were kids."

Her mouth falls open again. "What? But... but you never even spoke to me when we were younger."

"Yeah, I was morbidly timid around you. Lifelong crush and all that." I finish, smiling tenderly. Looking into her beautiful eyes, and trying to convey all I can't yet express with words.

She sighs and shakes her head almost imperceptibly, still not convinced. "Are you talking to any other women?"

My spine straightens at the insult. "Absolutely not, and before you ask: that has never even happened before."

Her beautiful, big brown eyes widen further, and I have to roll in my lips to control my amusement.

"I've been serious about you for a very long time, and I always hoped you might like me."

Hadeel sucks air between her teeth. "Don't be coy, you know I liked you. I spent my childhood chasing after you."

"But then you became a distant teenager and an even more detached young lady," I volley back. "Actually, I should be the one doubting your intentions."

Hadeel gifts me her first smile since I parked in from of her house almost a half hour ago. "But I haven't stated my intentions for you, brother," she teases in a saucy voice.

I take a step closer, our chests almost brushing. "What are your intentions toward me, Hadeel?" I ask with a sideways grin.

"I intend to get to know you and make up my mind if I'm keeping

41

you or not," she deadpans. Then, swirls on her heels, calling over her shoulder: "*Eid Mubarak*, brother. Now, come talk to my parents."

***

When we walk into Hadeel's parents' home, a little tornado bumps into my legs. I catch the precious little girl by her upper arms and set her straight.

"Careful, *habibti*."

"Sorry, uncle. Salaam!" She yells and takes off in another mad dash, a second girl coming to run after her.

"Sukeyna, Assyah! You girls better not make me come after you... *Ya Rabbi*!" Halima, Hadeel's older sister calls after who I assume are her two hellions.

I smile in amusement.

"*A Salaam U Aleykum*, Habib. Long time no see, brother. How've you been?"

"*Wu Aleykum A Salaam*, Halima. It's been a while, indeed. I'm great, *Hamdullah*, and you?"

"Can't complain, *MashAllah*. Those two keep me busy."

I chuckle again. "I can see that."

She shakes her head, *"SubhanAllah,"* then turns to a tall, imposing, blond and blue eyed, bearded man standing at her side. "This is my husband, Abdu Rahman."

We exchange a hug, salaams and smiles.

"Ah, Habib! *A Salaam U Aleykum,* my boy!" Mr. Seydi exclaims, coming to join our huddle in the foyer.

"Wu Aleykum A Salaam, uncle. It's good to see you." I move forward for an embrace.

Hadeel's dad greets me with affectionate slaps on my shoulder, then holds on to my hand, teasing: "you sure took your time..."

"Papa!" Hadeel exclaims and everyone else, including me, laughs.

Mrs. Seydi comes out of the open kitchen with Halima's daughters in tow, wiping at her eyes. "Salaam, Habib," she greet in a tremulous voice.

I return her salute with a warm smile, as Hadeel walks to her and wraps an arm around her shoulders.

"Awww, Mama," Halima coos and joins her mother and sister in a group hug.

"Come on, boys," Mr. Seydi calls, walking through the house and motioning for Abdu Rahman and myself to follow.

When we make it to the backyard, he invites us to take a seat on the comfortable outdoor furniture while the grill heats up for their *Eid* barbecue.

"Your father called me, Habib," Mr. Seydi opens the conversation.

I look up from my hands folded on my lap and smile. "I'm glad he did, uncle. I think you know what brings me today."

He nods without a word and I feel Abdu Rahman's sharp gaze study me.

"I'm ready to become a husband and a father, *Insha Allah.* I've always liked Hadeel, and I know it's not a coincidence we found ourselves in the same city, *MashAllah.*"

I mark a brief pause, letting my words penetrate.

"I've spoken to Hadeel and I'm hoping to get your blessing to court her, uncle."

He nods solemnly, a mist in his dark brown eyes, Hadeel's eyes.

"I'd be honored, son."

Abdu Rahman slaps my back loudly and booms through a chuckle: "*Mabruk*, brother!"

6

COURTING

HADEEL

Eleven hours, *Ya Rabbi*! When the plane finally lands, I grab my backpack and carry-on and speed-walk in direction of customs. *Hamdullah*, we're arriving on a Tuesday afternoon so the lines are not bad. Things go just as fast at the conveyor belt: my suitcase arrives in no time. I rush out of arrivals, already pulling out my phone to order a ride-share, when a voice I'd recognize anywhere calls for me.

"Habibti!"

My eyes fly from the cell phone screen to search the crowd, and I almost swoon when I see Habib standing there. Tall, broad and beaming. Looking like an oasis after days of not seeing him and the long cross-Atlantic flight . I bring my hands to my face, shaking my head, then advance toward him. Once I reach Habib, we stand toe to toe, drowning into each other's gazes, silly enamored grins on our faces. Not touching, not kissing

45

or even embracing like other couples are doing around us. Not holding hands. Just staring, taking in the other person, rejoicing in their presence.

"*A Salaam U Aleykum*, Habib."

"*Wu Aleykum A Salaam*," he replies, trading my carry-on for a bouquet of white roses.

My eyes grow big and I giggle.

"Quiet, I'm courting."

I laugh harder, as Habib takes hold of both my luggage and makes for the exit, throwing over his shoulder: "it's good to see you." A beautiful smile adorning his handsome face.

I trot behind him, nose buried in my flowers, and answer with a heartfelt: "good to see *you.*"

Habib shakes his head, chuckling.

"What?" I inquire.

"We're going to be one of those couples."

"Which ones?" I cannot contain my wide grin.

"The disgustingly happy ones," he replies, making me burst with laughter.

***

Turns out, my mom gave Mrs. Adam my flight details after I refused to share them with Habib. I didn't want him to bother with a trip to the airport on a work day, but apparently no one listens to me, and thank God for that!

When we make it to my place, Habib parks his Porsche Panamera in my building's underground lot and carries my luggage to the apartment.

In the elevator, I tease him, but also kind of want to know: "is this how it's going to be? Me not lifting a finger?"

He watches me closely, before asking in a serious tone: "does your mom carry her own suitcases?"

I dip my chin. "Point taken."

At my door, I start worrying about what might happen now... Habib pushes the suitcases past the threshold and stands in the hallway, hands stuffed in his pockets.

"Would you like to meet later for dinner?"

"You're not coming in?" I ask.

He shakes his head. "It's best I let you refresh and rest."

A mixture of relief and disappointment fills my heart.

47

"I'm probably just gonna order something and crash. Rain check on dinner?"

"OK. What do you feel like? I can put in the order while you get situated."

The lingering smile that's been on my face since I saw him at the airport grows up a notch.

"I'll be fine, honey."

At the endearment, both our pairs of eyes grow wide. It came out naturally, and he did call me *Habibti...*

"I'm leaving, now. Please call or text me when you're available. I believe we need to talk."

"About what?" I ask Habib's departing form.

"A lot of things," he replies with a wink before disappearing in the elevator.

Oh boy!

*** ***

HABIB

Two freaking weeks we've been back from California, and I

haven't seen Hadeel again since picking her up at the airport! First we both had to catch up on work, then I had a conference I needed to attend in Zurich. When I returned, she's the one who had a business trip in Dublin. Although I know this is nobody's fault, I'm seriously losing patience, and starting to wonder what type of married life we'll have. Even if we lived together, we would not have been able to see much of each other this past fortnight. And that worries me. I know Hadeel loves her job and so do I mine. I just don't see what type of compromise we can come up with. I rub the heels of my palms over my eyes and grab my phone, about to make our nightly call when it rings in my hand.

"*Salaam*, I was about to call you," I greet, trying to infuse warmth in my voice.

"*A Salaam U Aleykum*. What's wrong?" Is her response.

"What do you mean?"

"I can hear it in your voice, Habib. Something's bothering you."

MashAllah, this woman! I push through my doubts and fears, and ask: "is this how it's going to be when we're married?"

"What do you mean, hon'?"

"Both always busy outside our home, not having much time for one another," I elaborate.

Hadeel stays quiet for a beat.

49

"Sometimes, probably. But, we'll be more flexible once married."

"How?" I ask in a voice laden with frustration, and I want to kick myself for talking this way to my Hadeel.

In a soothing tone, she continues: "I can come with you when you have a conference and work from the hotel. Would you be able to do the same when I go on business trips?"

The giant weight that was resting on my chest seems to lift away in an instant, and I grumble: "probably."

Hadeel giggles. "Why are you still grumpy? I just addressed your concerns."

"Still haven't seen you in weeks," I retort.

"Then come see me," her sultry voice tempts me.

"Hadeel..." I warn.

"Not at my place, you perv'. There's a coffee shop down my street, they close late."

"Text me the address," I order and hang up. Sweeping my jacket and keys from the entrance, I get going, direction Hadeel's street.

***

This was a terrible idea. The second Hadeel walked into the cafe, wearing a long flowy dress, a silky hijab adorning her lovely face, beaming at my sight, I knew I was in trouble... And sure enough, things just went down from there. Mesmerized by the movement of her lips, I can barely understand what Hadeel is saying, and she has to keep repeating herself. My leg bounces under the table in a frantic motion, hands gripping my knees to refrain from touching her. I take deep inhales of the air around us, saturated with her flowery aroma. I can't wait to discover if the smell of flowers comes from her perfume, shampoo, lotion or some other cosmetic. *Ya Rabbi*, give me strength!

I've been fasting for days, making *dua* and nighttime prayer, but none of it tames my urges. I never felt this way. Yes, I've been attracted to other girls throughout my youth then later on other women, but I never doubted my ability to control myself. And that's exactly what's happening with Hadeel: I'm not sure I can keep it in check.

In an impulse, I lay my hand over hers resting on the table. Hadeel's eyes grow huge, but she doesn't break the contact. Her gaze goes from our joined hand to my face. she watches me with fascination, studying the hunger in my intense stare.

"We need to talk, *habibti*," I let out in a low tone.

She just bats her lashes, attentive at my every move. Not scared, not about to leave, but curious, fascinated.

"I know we agreed to wait till our trip home for *Eid Al Adha* to have the wedding, but I don't think that's going to work for me."

51

As soon as I see the glint of fear in Hadeel's eyes, I want to punch myself. And now she's about to bolt. I shake my head vehemently: "no, sweetheart. Look at me. I can't wait another month and a half. We have to get married sooner. I need you to be my wife."

Hadeel's mouth falls open in the cutest of 'Os' and I instantly grow hard. Yeah, there's no way.

"Can you take a week off?"

She shakes her head, eyes still dazed.

"Not for another month. We're closing a big deal, and I already requested the week of Eid. I can move it closer, but it's only going to be by a week or two max."

I grind my teeth and feel my jaw contract painfully.

"That will do," I growl, an absolute Neanderthal tonight.

Throwing a few bills on the table, I stand and motion for Hadeel to precede me. When we make it to her building entrance, I stay on the stairs and watch her intently.

"I'm sorry for my behavior. The wait is driving me crazy. I need to have you by my side."

I run a rough hand over my short cropped hair and Hadeel observes me with attention. Her gaze tender, understanding, full of a love I want to soak in and taste...

"It's okay, honey. We're almost there, *Insha Allah*. And just so you know, it's hard for me too."

"Not helping," I tease her and she giggles. The exquisite sound, music to my ears. "Now, go and let me know as soon as you have your new dates. I'll change mine accordingly and we'll let our families know."

"Yes, sir!" She mocks me.

"You're so lucky," I groan out, and Hadeel laughs again.

*** ***

HADEEL

'Salaam, habibti.'

My stomach dips at the way too familiar message, from a number that should not be texting me.

'Stop contacting me, Reda. I'm getting married in a week.' *Ya Allah*, help me! This man is going to get me in trouble.

The phone rings in my hand, making me jump. *SubhanAllah!*

"Are you kidding me, right now?" He yells in my ear. "You made me wait around for almost a year, and now you're getting married? A month after you dumped me?"

53

"Calm down, Reda. Don't make me regret I took your call."

"I'll show you regret, you..."

At the string of curses that follows, I hang up, my eyes filling with tears.

I haven't told Habib that Reda started texting me again after Ramadan. First, it was a cordial: *'Eid Mubarak'*, to which I responded in a short but friendly manner. Then he started sending me messages every couple of days, asking how my day went, what I was doing. I'd hoped my perfunctory answers would discourage him, but Reda didn't seem to mind my dismissive tone. So, finally last week I got tired of his shenanigans and told him I was engaged. Hoping this would put an end to his desperate behavior. It didn't. Reda's stupid answer was: *'Well, you're not married yet.'* From that day on, I took a different approach and started ignoring his messages.

I wanted to kill him! And myself, for being so dumb and getting in such a messy situation. My first mistake had been to speak to a man without my parents' permission, even if he was respectful, vouched for by a close friend and made his good intentions clear. And now, I was getting muddled in a stupid situation that could only bring trouble in my relationship.

But today, I'm meeting Habib and can't have this jerk blow off my phone while I'll be with my future husband. That's why I was upfront and told him something that's actually none of his business.

Before leaving my place, I make *dua* and promise myself to call my mother and sister about this mess.

***

"All the details have finally been settled," I smile huge at Habib, sipping on my tea, sitting at our usual spot at the café terrace.

"*Alhamdulilah. Jazak Allahu Hayran*, future wife."

I shake my head at what Habib has been calling me lately.

"*Insha Allah*, brother," I poke fun at him.

"*Insha Allahu Rabbi*, indeed."

We get lost into each other's gaze, daydreaming about our upcoming nuptials. When a male voice shatters our bliss.

"Ah there you are, *habibti*." Reda calls from the sidewalk, and I freeze.

He's standing a few feet away from us, a nasty grin on his face, holding a huge bouquet of flowers. Clearly up to no good.

"*A Salaam U Aleykum*, brother." Reda walks to Habib, arm extended.

Habib rises from his seat and shakes the offered hand. "*Wu Aleykum A Salaam*," my fiancé responds with a suspicious glance at the stranger facing him.

Reda pulls a chair and sits at our table, dropping the flowers in front of me.

"These are for you, love," he says.

I stiffen in my chair and turn to Habib to see his alarmed eyes bounce between Reda and I. I have no clue what to do.

"I'm guessing you know who I am," Reda taunts Habib with a smirk.

"No, man. I don't know you," comes out gruff.

"Reda?" He questions.

Habib shakes his head, lips pinched, brow furrowed, and I can see a muscle jump in his cheek as his temper rises. *Allahu Akbar!*

"I'm the ex," the scumbag introduces himself.

When Habib doesn't respond, just sits there burning a hole into Reda's face, the arrogant pig adds: "we dated for almost a year. I was about to introduce her to my parents. I'd be careful if I were you, man. She doesn't know what she wants."'

Still complete silence from Habib and I'm too shocked to utter a word.

"Did she tell you we've been talking again since *Eid?*"

"You need to leave," Habib snarls.

56

And Reda laughs... laughs! Does he not see how furious my man is? How his hands are balling into fists, his feet frantically tapping the pavement? Face rigid as granite... This guy must be suicidal! Habib is clearly taller and much bigger then Reda.

"Brother," Habib spits out in an absolutely unbrotherly tone, "you can leave now or I'll make you."

Reda chuckles maniacally, but when Habib stands to his full stature, his face scrunches up in a nasty snarl and he pushes his chair back abruptly.

"Fine, I'll leave. You can have my leftovers."

Habib grabs the flowers from the table, fists Reda's collar and throws him on the ground in a succession of swift motions. Then, he comes to stand right above to the poor guy, the points of his Italian loafers close to Reda's heaving chest.

"We never see or hear from you again, yeah?"

When Reda doesn't respond, too busy scrambling back to his feet and arranging his clothes, Habib advances on him and asks again, low and menacing: "yeah?"

Face pinched and red, hair a mess, and altogether looking pathetic, Reda stares at Habib for a beat before accepting his defeat and nodding once. Then, he turns on his heels and walks away as fast as his jerky steps allow.

My eyes come back to Habib and I flinch at the mask of cold fury they encounter. I stand from my chair, extending a hand

57

and start in an appeasing voice: "Habib..."

He interrupts me with a curt: "not here," and throws a wad of bills on the table.

I shoulder my purse and start walking in the direction of my building, head bent to hide my tear-streaked face. *Ya Rabbi, what have I done?*

Habib's steps resonate on the pavement, at a slight distance from me. From my peripheral vision, I can discern his tall, strong form, hands stuffed in his pockets, body rigid. I just don't know if it's with anger, disappointment, hurt... Probably all of it. *How could I have been so stupid?*

I'm surprised when Habib doesn't bid me farewell at my building entrance, but silently follows up the lift, then to my door. The air is heavily charged with tension, and we still haven't look at each another.

Once the door's unlocked, I gather a strengthening breath and turn to face him, blurting out: "I can explain."

Eyes drowned in sadness, he replies: "you should have done that before."

I try insisting: "Habib, I..."

"No, Hadeel. What just happened was not OK. I need a minute to digest. I'll see you at home, in a week. We'll talk, then."

My watery eyes grow wide and I ask in a broken voice: "we'll...

talk?"

He nods, gaze inscrutable. "Give me a week, *habibti*."

I let out an involuntary sob and Habib flinches, before rubbing at his own redden eyes. Then, he walks away...

7

HOME

HADEEL

I run the tips of my fingers over the shiny ring on my finger. An eighteen carats gold band and huge, glinting diamond. The one Habib and I chose together at a time when it seemed nothing could shake us. The image of our blissful, clueless happiness flashes behind my eyes, and I tilt my head up, pushing back the tears... again.

I've been open with my family and Huda about what played out between Reda, Habib and I. As I expected, no one blamed me. They could tell how much I was already beating myself, and probably also felt for me, and understood I found myself in an impossible position I wasn't equipped to deal with.

Habib? I haven't heard from. In a week. The man who said he'd been serious about me for a long time. The same one who started courting me within weeks of us being reunited. The guy who couldn't wait a couple of months to get married to me. The one who's ignored all my messages, and hasn't taken a single one of my calls in seven days.

I bring my hands together, palms open and whisper a prayer that's a balm to my sore heart. *May Allah keep my home safe in my absence, grant me a fruitful trip, make the best for me, in this life and the next one, and may He grant the same to all His creation, ameen.* I've always put my faith in Our Lord and this time won't be any different.

***

"*A Salaam U Aleykum, habibti,*" my father greets, wrapping me in his arms.

He squeezes a bit stronger than usual, as if he hasn't seen me just a month ago, or as if to put back together the pieces of my shattered heart... I hold him just as tight, inhaling his familiar scent: musk and Head & Shoulders. The most comforting scent in the world.

I cling on to my dad for much longer than I've done in more than a decade, then detach myself with a sniffling laugh.

"*Wu Aleykum A Salaam.* I'm sorry, Papa. I've been a mess, lately."

"It's OK, my sweet girl. I'm sure it hasn't been easy for Habib either."

I nod non-committally: I have not had very kind thoughts about Habib in recent days.

"Have you heard anything?" I inquire, trying not to express too much anguish in my words.

He shakes his head in a slow, miserable motion. It's impressive how witnessing their child's hurt affects a parent. My strong, always pragmatic dad seems at a loss.

"We respected your request to not mention anything to Habib's family. All we've communicated about are preparations for tomorrow, honey. They don't even seem to be aware there might be an issue."

You mean they don't seem to be aware there might not be a wedding... I think to myself, but don't say out loud.

Our couple of hours drive home from the San Francisco Airport is devoid of the usual incessant back and forth discussion and teasing. My father focuses on the road, while I let my eyes take in the mountains and valleys we pass. I miss home. The wide open spaces, nature, the quiet life of a small town. London is amazing, but now that I might go back to my lonely apartment and risk running into Habib, it has lost some of its charm...

As if reading my thoughts, my dad pats my knee, saying: "*Insha Alla*, all will be well."

I take in a deep inhale and nod. It will be, eventually. I just don't know how many tribulations I'll have to go through before my life becomes peaceful again.

***

Laying in my bed, eyes glued to the ceiling, I mentally trace the glow-in-the-dark constellations my dad glued for us when we were little girls. Over the years, some of the stars have fallen, just like in real life. Extinguished, gone. Beautiful miracles, forever lost to the world. Just like my union to Habib might be.

Get it together, Hadeel! He's not the only man on earth. there will be other opportunities. Plus, who says I have to marry for love? God, I sound pathetic to my own ears.

Lost in my thoughts, at first I don't notice the tapping sound on my window, till it becomes more frequent. Frowning, I get off the bed and advance to the panel, peeking outside for any sign of what could be making the noise. My parents live in a gated community, so I feel very safe and don't even consider the possibility of an intruder. Maybe a racoon?...

I almost trip over my feet when I see a tall figure, dressed in flannel pajamas and a gray cotton t-shirt, standing on the lawn, holding a handful of tiny pebbles he must have been throwing at my window. We stand there for a moment, Habib staring up into my window, me watching him with a strange mixture of apprehension and hope. His unreadable expression doesn't give away anything, and my insides churn with both anxiety and the relief of finally getting to see him.

I slip into my thick fleece robe and furry slippers, wrap a scarf around my head and hurry down the stairs as quietly as I can.

*** ***

HABIB

Hadeel sneaks out of her parents' home, a flawless vision of domesticity. She looks warm and cozy in her oversized plush robe, headwrap and slippers. All various shades of pink. I almost smile at the image she offers, cute and huggable. Almost.

She's not smiling at me, though. Her expression displays the hurt of her unanswered calls and messages, the worry about what our future entails. She also seems mad and maybe, God willing, hopeful...

She stops at a few feet distance from me.

"*A Salaam U Aleykum, Habib.*"

"*Wu Aleykum A Salaam*, Hadeel. How are you?"

My question ignites a flare of temper in her amber eyes.

"Fine, *Hamdullah.*"

I nod and take a step forward, unable to maintain the excruciating distance I've imposed on us for the past week.

"Not me," I whisper. "I'm not doing fine."

She lets out a broken exhale, emboldening me, and I further close the distance between us. Coming to stand so near that the heat of our bodies mingle in the soft summer night. I stop before the temptation to take her hand becomes too strong.

"I messed up," I admit.

64

Hadeel faintly shakes her head and moves closer. "No, I messed up. It's just... I didn't know how to tell you..."

Heartbroken by the image of my strong, beautiful intended fidgeting her hands, and at her anguish filled voice, I interrupt: "No, Hadeel. I messed up." I bend my knees to bring our faces level, intently gazing into her eyes. "I was hurt, jealous and furious at that prick and the situation we found ourselves into."

When she looks away, eyes filled with tears, my fingers lift of their own accord and wrap around her chin, turning her face back to me.

"You did nothing wrong, *habibti*." My voice is low and soft. Full of remorse. Gentle enough to soothe. Asking for forgiveness.

Hadeel's big brown eyes stare up at me, tears rolling down her face.

"This was a bump on our path. A lesson. We have to talk to each other. That's it. I trust you. I know you... and I love you."

She lets out a soft sob, at once breaking and mending my heart.

"I'm so very sorry I hurt you. I... I couldn't... didn't want to say or do something I wouldn't be able to take back. I'm sorry, honey."

Hadeel wipes away at her face and gives me a brave, shaky smile. "I appreciate you taking ownership of your part of responsibility and I forgive you, but I'm at fault too. I should never have been talking to Reda or seeing him without a proper introduction to

65

my family. And I, especially, should never have allowed him to keep contacting me after you and I got engaged."

In a gesture mirroring my earlier one, she cups my jaw into her soft, warm palm, asking: "forgive me?"

Throat constricted, I can only nod my acquiescement and Hadeel's smile blooms into full life.

"You cannot do this, Habib. You also have to talk to me."

I nod again, frantically this time, words still stuck down my throat.

"Good, now go get some rest. We have a big day tomorrow, *Insha Allah*" Hadeel concludes, having regained her spunk.

I let out a constricted chuckle. "Okay, I'll let you rest, too. Good night, *habibti*."

As she's about to get back inside I call: "Hadeel."

She turns around, gifting me a tender smile at odds with her whisper-shouted: "what?"

"Tomorrow at this time, you'll be all mine *Insha Allah*."

I watch in the dim light of the street lamp, as heat creeps up her cheeks. Then she hurries inside, making me chuckle.

*** ***

66

<u>HADEEL</u>

"*Ya Rabbi*, child stop fidgeting!" My mother admonishes me in a mocking tone.

"Leave her alone, Ma," Halima comes to my rescue, also snickering.

"I hate you both," I grumble through the side of my mouth, trying and failing to let the makeup artist finish her work without moving too much.

She smiles indulgently, taking a step back to admire her handiwork. "Leave the girl alone," she points the brush held through her fingers to Halima. "I still remember how much of a mess you were on your wedding day."

My sister bursts with laughter and I follow suit. I don't know if this is the best day of my life, but it sure is close to perfection, *MashAllah*!

After a week of absolute misery, all I've experienced since last night is happiness. And I look forward to the conclusion of this amazing day, *Alhamdulilah*. Our wedding ceremony was officiated by the *imam* who taught us *Quran* and has known Habib and I for most of our lives. His smile was full of warmth and brought even more tears to my eyes.

Habib looked dashing in the traditional *Daara* of his parents' native Mauritania, and I wore a gorgeous Senegalese tunic in homage to my family's home country. I felt amazing, princess-like. Hair done in a sophisticated fashion under my veil-like hijab, intricate henna designs on my hands and feet, surrounded by my loved ones. Even Huda flew home, leaving her poor husband and son to fend for themselves for a weekend, *MashAllah*.

The entire day was beyond perfect, and now I can't wait for the private party between my husband and I!

"Nervous?" Maman asks, once the makeup artist has left and it's only the three of us. Knocked out by jet lag and her cumulated sleep deprivation, Huda was resting at her parents'.

I shake my head, a beaming smile illuminating my face: "no, I'm just excited."

My mom turns to my sister and they explode in another fit of laughter.

I feel my cheeks turn hot and cry out: "that's not what I meant!"

They laugh again, and Ma comes to wrap an arm around my shoulders. She takes my hand and presses a soft kiss at its back.

"Be excited as much as you want and for every aspect of your marriage, my love. *Alhamdulilah*, *Allah* blessed you with love, just like me and your sister. I'm so very happy for you."

The sheen in my eyes threatens to roll down my face and I look up to the ceiling, blinking back the tears. "Stop it, Ma!"

"Okay, it's almost time. Any questions?" Halima asks with a

malicious twinkle in her gaze.

I shake my head, rolling my eyes.

"Good, let's get you downstairs before Habib arrives."

***

I press my palms on my heated cheeks and take a deep inhale, watching my reflection in the bathroom mirror. I look like a glamorized version of myself, with the straightened and curled hair, subtle but enticing makeup, and more than anything else, the molding, lacy nightgown, unlike anything I've ever worn in my life. But I feel, beautiful, powerful, at peace, excited and ready to fully become Habib's wife.

*** ***

HABIB

Eyes on my toes digging into the plush carpet, I try to keep my mind from the noises coming from the closed door.

Images of today start running through my mind: the ceremony, the reception attended by our families and so many of our childhood friends. The hours spent sitting next to Hadeel, holding hands under the table. Finally free to touch each other at will, but our movements limited by the small crowd surrounding us. All the joy and blessings we were able to share with our loved ones, *MashAllah*. A wistful smile adorns my face.

69

The door to the bathroom opens, revealing a vision. My wife might just be the most beautiful and sexiest thing I've ever laid eyes on. She glides toward the hotel suite's California King size bed, where I'm sitting. A gorgeous smile brightening her beautiful features, body encased in lace that hugs her so close, it seems painted on. My mouth goes dry and I stand abruptly, closing the distance between us in one swift stride. I grab Hadeel, one hand wrapped at the back of her neck and the other one tight at her incurved waist, whisper a soft prayer against her lips and land my mouth on hers...

8

EPILOGUE

HABIB

I don't understand women. Hadeel brought all her things from California to our Queensbridge townhouse. Everything. We moved in a month ago, and I'm still unpacking Mrs. Adam's boxes. *Unbelievable*, I think to myself with a sideways grin.

The box I'm currently working on is an incomprehensible assortment of trinkets. So far, I've unwrapped a snowball, a couple of sports trophies and a few more of her beloved romance novels... None of this would have followed me. I don't think I've ever owned a snowball, my trophies are stuffed somewhere in a storage, and I usually don't keep books I've already read.

A delicious aroma wafts its way from the kitchen, where my dear wife is making dinner. The soft sounds of a jazz playlist fill the open kitchen and the living room where I'm sitting on the carpet.

This is the life. A good, beautiful, loving woman as my life companion, *MashAllah*. Our love, friendship, affection, mutual trust and easy camaraderie making our house into a home. *Hamdullah*, we are so blessed.

Mind filled with happy thoughts, I keep digging into Hadeel's treasure box. At the very bottom, my fingers encounter a hard, rectangular shape, wrapped in newspaper. I rip away the paper to reveal a small frame, maybe the size of one of my large hands. Inside the frame, a piece of paper is trapped. White page, with a single sentence scribbled in... my handwritting.

"Hadeel!"

"Yes, habibi. Once second, please."

My gaze travels from the frame that for all these years has kept safe the note I forgot about, to my gorgeous wife wiping her hands on a kitchen towel and walking toward me in a hypnotizing movement of her full hips. I'm still not used to seeing her in the tight jeans and form-fitting dresses reserved for my eyes.

Shaking out of it, I extend my arm, pulling Hadeel down on the carpet next to me, and place the frame in her hands.

She gasps softly, eyes getting misty, then lifts her face to mine. "It's your handwriting!"

I nod, pulling her into my arms. holding on tight and resting my chin on top of her head. Expressing all the love I wish I could have given that young girl. The one who was brave and didn't take the easy path. The one who used to cautiously watch me from afar, till she lost faith in the possibility of an us.

"Did it help, even a little?" I ask quietly.

Hadeel nods against my chest, before lifting her face and dropping a tender kiss on my lips. Her soft hands coming up to frame my face.

"More than you'll ever know, my love."

I take her mouth in a deep, loving, passionate kiss, and we let our bodies express a bond beyond words. I make a quick *dua* of gratitude and pray for our love and its fruits to stay eternally blessed.

THE END

About the Author

Seyna Rytes can't remember a time when she wasn't daydreaming love stories (long before she learnt how to write them!), watching romantic movies (The Princess Bride, anyone?), or reading romance (from vintage Harlequin to contemporary smut...). Seyna lives on the Central Coast of California with her husband & their kids and strives to tell the stories inspired by her West African & French origins!

You can connect with me on:
- https://seynarytes.wixsite.com/website
- https://twitter.com/SRytes
- https://www.facebook.com/SeynaWritesDiverseRomance

Subscribe to my newsletter:
- http://eepurl.com/gT4Cv1

Also by Seyna Rytes

Fun, heartfelt, diverse romance!

Seven Days To Love: : Falling For The Johnsons Book 1 (A Sweet, Big Brother's Best Friend, Short Romance)
Deejah Johnson has been in love with her childhood neighbor, and big brother's best friend for most of her life, but Kareem has never even kissed her. After almost two decades of waiting in vain, Deejah's set on forgetting the big hunk of a man, and moving on with her life. And, of course, that's the moment Kareem chooses to start showing her interest.

Follow Kareem and Deejah in this sweet story set during Black History Month, as their families come together to celebrate unity.

Will the eternally quiet girl stand up for herself? Is Kareem finally gonna get his head straight and claim her heart? Will their families stop mingling in their business?

Made in the USA
Las Vegas, NV
08 July 2022